Gingerbread Boy

by Liza Charlesworth

ISBN: 978-0-545-25644-5

Illustrated by Anne Kennedy
Designed by Maria Lilja • Colored by Ka-Yeon Kim-Li
Copyright © 2010 by Liza Charlesworth
All rights reserved. Published by Scholastic Inc. Printed in China.

Let's make a gingerbread boy.

First, I put on two eyes.

Then, I put on one nose.

Then, I put on one mouth.

Then, I put on four buttons.

Then, I put on two ears.

Hey! Come back here!